MY FIRST SNOW DAY

By

Faridat A. Audu

Copyright © 2025
Faridat A. Audu

ISBN
979-8-89795-224-3
979-8-89795-225-0
979-8-89795-226-7

Dedicated To

All my extended family and friends for their support and words of encouragement at all times. Thank you!

&

To Kelly Holohan, this book's title inspiration came from your Grade 1 classroom. Thank You!

"Madame Enns, what is a snow day?" Atai curiously asked his teacher during class.

DAYS OF THE WEEK
MONDAY
TUESDAY
WEDNESDAY
THURSDAY
FRIDAY
SATURDAY
SUNDAY

MONTHS OF THE YEAR
JANUARY
FEBRUARY
MARCH
APRIL
JULY
AUGUST
SEPTEMBER

MATH

Madame Enns smiled and said, "A snow day is when a lot of snow or ice falls on the ground, and it becomes unsafe for cars and buses to drive or bring children to school. So, most schools would be closed, and students would have to stay home."

Atai was happy to hear that he would stay home
for more playtime with his baby brother Ayegba
but sad that he would miss his school friends

However, he was excited to experience his first snow day. The next morning, Ataï's mama dressed him up for the weather with his winter gadgets, and they had so much fun in the snow.

Atai built a snowman with a carrot nose and big eyes and made snow angels with his family. He loved it so much that he happily asked Mama if it could be a snow day every day.

"Unfortunately, snow doesn't fall every day but only during winter," Ataï's papa explained. Ataï's mama and papa showed him how to make a snow fort, and they worked together to build it.

Atai and his papa packed the snow tightly and made sure it was strong enough to with stand any snowball attacks. Atai was proud of the fort he helped build, and he couldn't wait to have a snowball fight with his family.

They had a great time playing in the snow, and Atai's mama and papa taught him about the different types of snowflakes and how to catch them on his tongue.

Atai was amazed at how each snowflake was unique, and he spent a long time trying to catch as many as he could. When it was time to go back inside, Atai was sad to leave the snow behind.

He didn't want the fun to end, but he was also excited to warm up inside with a cup of hot chocolate. He asked his mother for another one and she smiled. "You really love hot chocolate don't you, my dear," she said. Atai was delighted to get his second cup. Wouldn't it be better if every day was a snow day, Atai thought.

"I had so much fun, Mama and Papa! Thank you for taking me out in the snow," Atai said, beaming with joy.

"We're glad you had a good time, Atai. Always remember to dress warmly when it's cold outside and be careful when playing outside, especially when the ground is slippery," Atai's mama reminded him.

He spent the rest of the day indoors sitting on his
father's lap as he read him a storybook.

Later in the evening, Atai spent time with his younger brother, Ayegba.

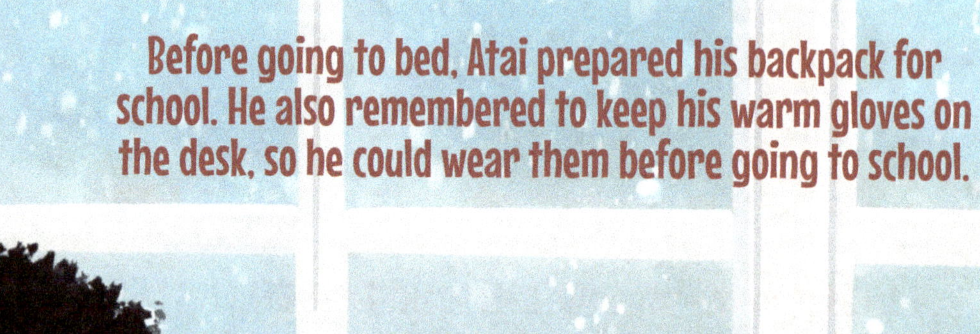

Before going to bed, Atai prepared his backpack for school. He also remembered to keep his warm gloves on the desk, so he could wear them before going to school.

Atai went to bed that night, dreaming of his next snow day. He knew that it might not come for a while, but he was excited to experience it again.

He couldn't wait to build another snowman, make more snow angels, and have another snowball fight with his family.

Atai also dreamt that he was playing in the snow with his school friends. He saw that he made a snowman with them the same way he made it with his family.

The next morning, Atai woke up and looked out the window, hoping to see more snow. It wasn't snowing but he saw the ground was packed with snow.
It looked as if the ground had been covered by a huge white blanket. It was still really chilly, enough to give him the jitters!

Atai was excited that he could wear his warm clothes today as well.

As he got ready for school, Atai put on his warm clothes, he put on everything himself this time and learnt how to properly wear his gear.

As he set foot outside, the feeling of the cold wind on his face made him excited. The snow made a crunching sound under his boots and sparkled in the sunlight.

When Atai arrived at school, he couldn't find his friends in the class-room. "Madame Enns, where are my friends? Why aren't they here today?" Atai asked his teacher.

"Ah, they are outside, my dear. They are busy playing in the snow on the school playground. Go and play with them," Madame Enns said.

Atai ran outside excitedly to play with his friends. He was delighted to find Tokunbo and Asim both waiting for him with small shovels in their hands, so that they could play in the snow and build stuff. Tokunbo and Asim were his best friends. They got along very well and enjoyed each other's company.

Atai realized that he was lucky to have had a fun
snow day with his family and friends.
He enjoyed a snowball fight and rolling around in
the snow. It was a day to remember.

From that day on, Atai always looked forward to the winter, hoping that he might get to experience another snow day.

He knew that he would be ready with his winter gear and a big smile on his face, ready to have more fun in the snow with his family and friends.

THE END

Books in the
MY FIRST... Series:

My First Word

My First Day in Kindergarten

My First Lost Tooth

My First Snow Day

My First Sleepover

All inquiries should be addressed to:
Global Vous Education INC. Canada
www.globalvouseducation.com

ABOUT THE AUTHOR

Faridat A. Audu is a Nigerian-Canadian early childhood educator with a Bachelor of Arts in English Language from Africa, a Professional Children's Writing Certificate from the USA, and a Master's degree in Educational Leadership from Canada. With an Award of Excellence in Early Childhood Education from Humber College and over 15 years of experience in the field, spanning Nigeria, Côte d'Ivoire, and Canada. Faridat is passionate about education and the founder of Global Vous Education INC., dedicated to fostering bilingualism and introducing contemporary educational trends with a focus on the Early Years and French language. Faridat is also the proud author of My First Approach to Being Bilingual, widely acclaimed for its invaluable guidance for English and French language learners.

Born in Lagos, Nigeria, Faridat has studied and traveled extensively worldwide. Currently, she resides in Ontario, Canada, with her husband and three sons. Her global perspective and dedication continue to inspire and empower educators, parents, and children alike.

ACTIVITY SECTION

Here are some fun activities that parents and educators could do with children. These activities would permit parents or educators to reflect on children's early years experiences in a fun, and interactive way.

(For Parents)

This activity is for parents. After reading "My First Snow Day" with your child, you can share with your children what their first snow day was like.

(For Educators)

This activity is for educators. As an educator, you can create classroom projects or exercises that would allow students to ask their parents about their first snow day and share it with their peers the next day in class.

HAVE FUN!

9 7 9 8 8 9 7 9 5 2 2 5 0